This 1989 edition published by Derrydale Books,
distributed by Crown Publishers, Inc.,
225 Park Avenue South
New York, N.Y. 10003

Directed by HELENA Productions Ltd.
Illustrated by Van Gool-Lefevre-Loiseaux

Produced by Twin Books
15 Sherwood Place
Greenwich, CT 06830
Printed in Spain by
Printer industria gráfica sa. Barcelona
D. L. B.: 26783-1989
ISBN 0-517-69320-8

hgfedcba

Jack and the Beanstalk

Twin Books

DERRYDALE BOOKS
New York

Jack and his widowed mother lived together in a small cottage in the forest. They had a spotted cow that gave rich milk—more than they could drink. So they made cheese and butter from the extra milk to sell at the market.

But one morning the cow went dry. There was no milk to drink and no food to sell. When Jack saw how worried his mother was, he stopped playing with his pet squirrel, Phil, and said: "It's all right, Mother. I'll take the cow to market and sell her. Then we'll have money to live on."

"We'll be back soon, Mother," called Jack, as he led the cow out of the yard. "We're sure to get a good price for our cow, so we won't go hungry."

Two birds had overheard him, and suddenly one of them called out, "We know where you can sell your cow!" Jack loved adventures, so he followed the birds into the forest.

The path showed by the birds led the little group to an old man leaning on a staff deep in the woods.

"So you want to sell that fine-looking cow, do you?" the old man asked, as one of the birds perched on his hat. "I'll take her gladly, in exchange for these magic beans." He showed Jack a handful of beautifully colored beans.

Jack was tempted by their brilliant colors—and by the word "magic." He handed over the cow's halter and ran home with the beans.

"Mother, look!" Jack cried, rushing into the cottage.

"What?" exclaimed his mother. "Have you sold the cow already?"

"Yes!" he said excitedly. "In exchange for these magic beans!"

But Jack's mother was very upset when she found he had gotten no money for the cow. "What will we live on?" she said angrily. "These are worthless!" And she threw the beans into the yard.

Jack and his mother went to bed sadly that night, after eating the last of their food.

But imagine Jack's surprise when one of the birds he had met the day before awakened him early in the morning. The bird showed him a vine so large that its leaves were bursting through his window! The magic beans his mother had thrown away had grown into an enormous beanstalk overnight!

Jack ran outside. The beanstalk reached so high above the cottage that it disappeared into the clouds. Eagerly, Jack began to climb. "Where do you think we'll end up, Phil? he asked. But Phil could only wonder, too.

The friends climbed higher and higher, until they reached a land above the clouds. In the distance they saw a great castle.

"Lets find out who lives there," said Jack. "Maybe they'll give us something to eat!" All these adventures were making him hungry.

Jack and his friends made
their way to the huge door of
the castle. "Is anyone home?"
shouted Jack. To his aston-
ishment, a giantess came to the
door and stared down at him.

"You're just the boy I need
to help with the housework!"
she said. "But come in quickly
and hide, before my husband
comes home, or he'll eat you up."

Jack's hunger overcame his fear, so he ran inside and hid under the dining room table. Then the giant's heavy footsteps shook the castle. Stamping into the room, he roared:

"Fee, fi, fo, fum,
I smell the blood of an Englishman;
Be he alive or be he dead
I'll grind his bones to make my bread!"

Jack shook with fright, but the giantess said to her husband: "You don't smell anything but the nice ox I've cooked for your dinner. Sit down and eat it while it's hot."

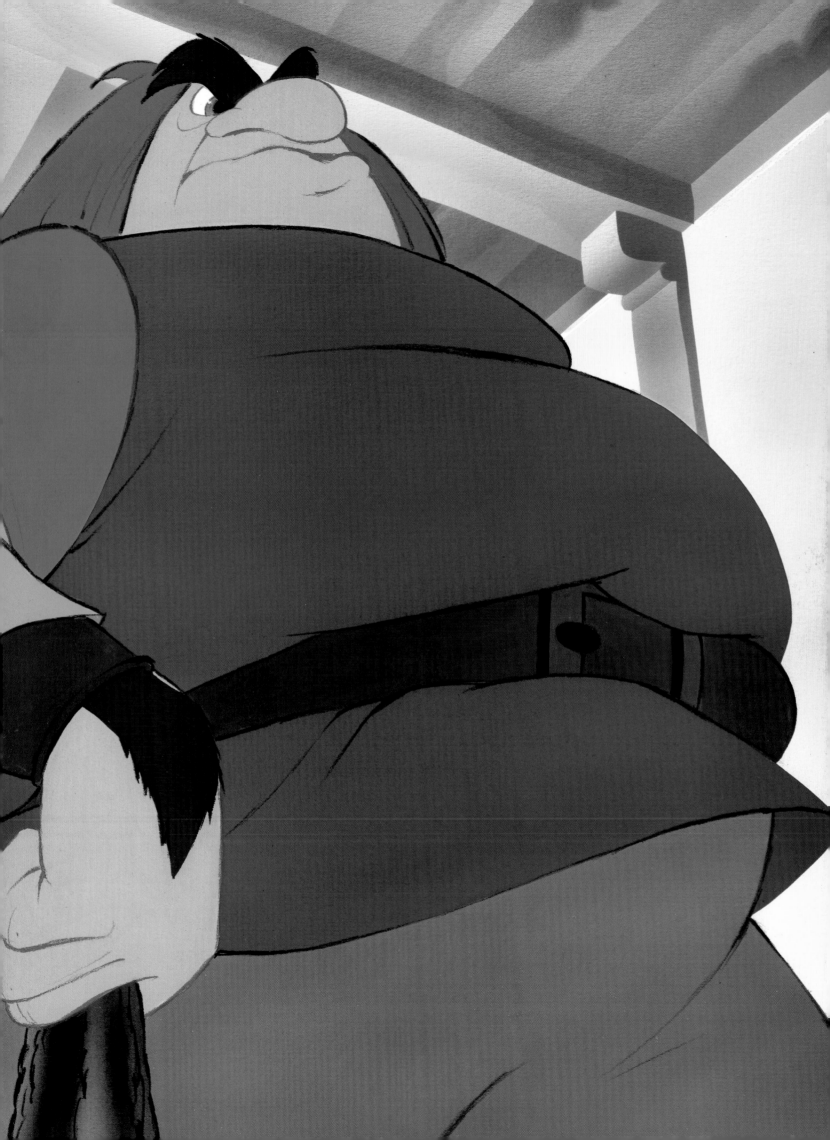

After the giant had eaten the entire ox, he called, "Wife, bring me my magic hen. I want to see her lay some golden eggs."

From his hiding place, Jack watched in disbelief, as the giant commanded the little hen to lay an egg. When she did, Jack saw that the egg glittered in the giant's hand like pure gold. Beside it shone a golden harp, another of the giant's treasures.

When the giant fell asleep at the table, Jack sprang out of hiding and seized the magic hen. With his heart hammering, he sped toward the window with the hen tucked under his arm.

The hen clucked with alarm when Jack and Phil leaped out the window. They raced across the plain toward the beanstalk.

When the hen saw how far it was to the ground, she squawked so loudly that Phil tried to hush her. He was afraid she would awaken the giant.

It was too late! The hen's outcry had already aroused the monster. His heavy tread shook the ground like an earthquake as he pursued them!

"That club of his could fell a tree!" cried Jack, as he and Phil scrambled down the beanstalk as fast as they could.

Jack's mother was so happy to see him back safe that she burst into tears. Then Jack showed her the magic hen and told her about the golden eggs.

"We need never be poor again, Mother," he said proudly. The little household was filled with rejoicing.

But Jack was too adventurous to stay quietly at home for long. He kept thinking of the giant's golden harp. One bright morning, he climbed the beanstalk again.

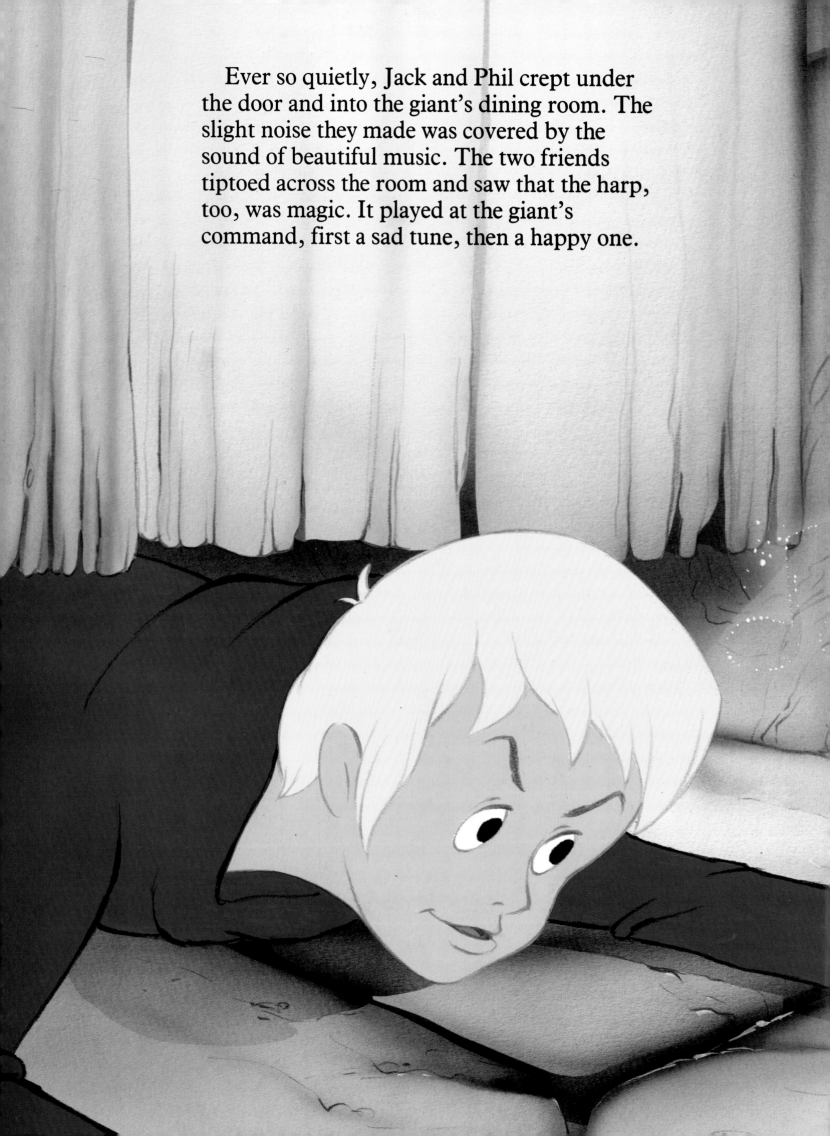

Ever so quietly, Jack and Phil crept under the door and into the giant's dining room. The slight noise they made was covered by the sound of beautiful music. The two friends tiptoed across the room and saw that the harp, too, was magic. It played at the giant's command, first a sad tune, then a happy one.

"Play again!" the giant ordered, and the harp responded with another burst of sweet music that filled the castle. Jack and Phil forgot about caution as they drew closer to listen. Suddenly, the giant spotted them!

"You stole my magic hen!" he roared, seizing his huge club. Jack snatched the harp and ran for his life, with Phil close behind.

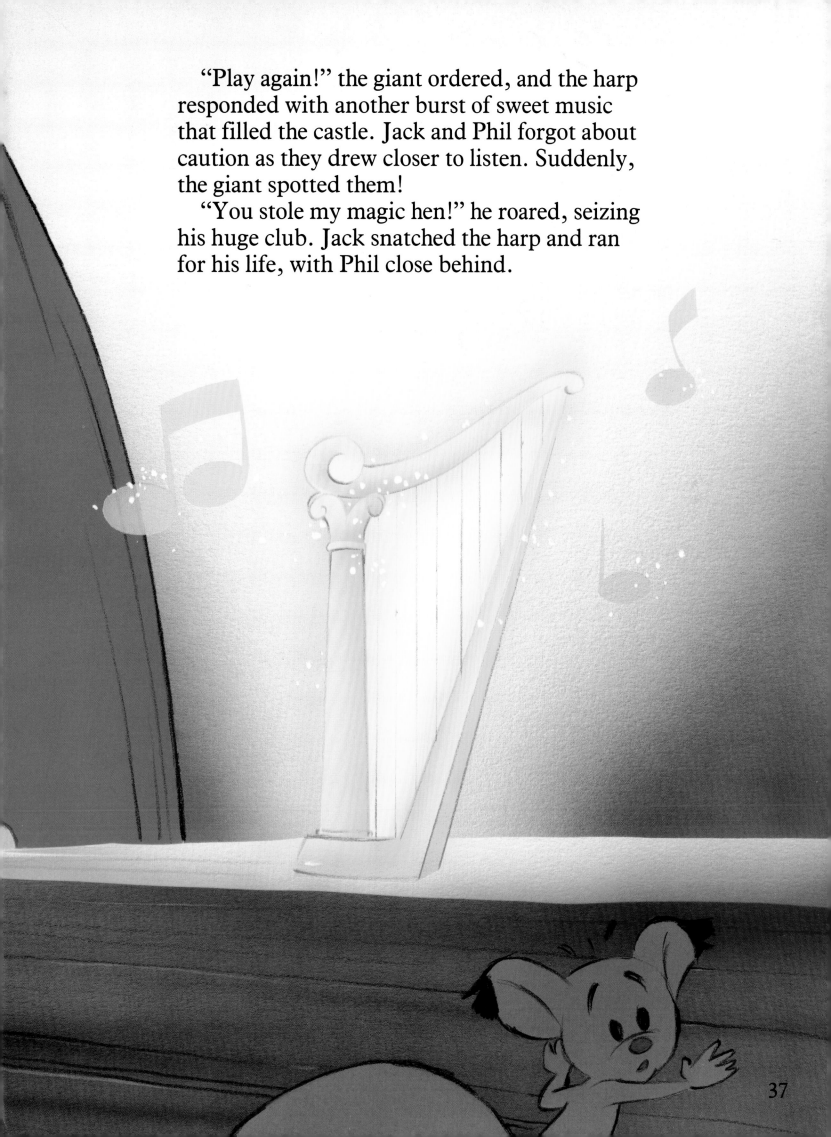

"Hurry!" cried their guide. "He's gaining on you!"

Jack and Phil reached the beanstalk and began to climb down. The magic harp was crying, "Master, master!" as the giant followed close behind them.

Luckily, their small size and weight made Jack and Phil much faster than the clumsy giant. They soon reached the ground, and Jack seized an axe and struck at the base of the beanstalk. He chopped with all his strength.

Just as it seemed the giant would catch up with them, the great beanstalk began to sway back and forth. Then, with a loud *crack*, it crashed to the ground. The giant fell with it and lay motionless.

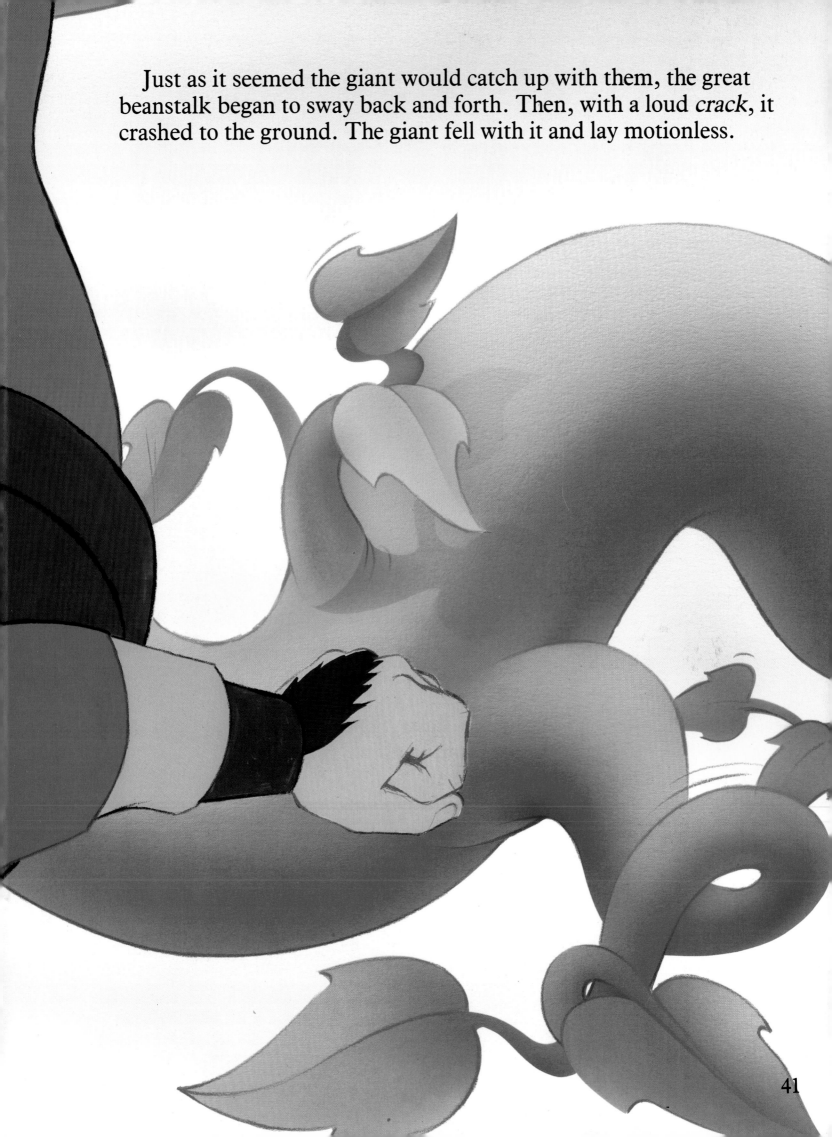

"Look, Mother!" cried Jack. "The giant will never frighten anyone again. And we've got his magic harp as well as the hen!"

With that, the faithful bird who had guided Jack through his adventures took flight, and Jack and his mother went into the cottage.

"What a brave, clever boy you are!" said Jack's mother, giving him a hug. "And how glad I am now that you went adventuring." And just as they should, they lived happily ever after.